CAPTAIN PEPPER'S PETS

SALLY GRINDLEY

ILLUSTRATED BY
DAVID PARKINS

KINGFISHER
BOSTON

To Chris and Richard Downs—S. G.

To the staff and children of
St. Faith's Infant School, Lincoln, England—D. P.

KINGFISHER
a Houghton Mifflin Company imprint
222 Berkeley Street
Boston, Massachusetts 02116
www.houghtonmifflinbooks.com

First published by Kingfisher in 2002
This edition published in 2004
2 4 6 8 10 9 7 5 3 1
1TR/0104/TWP/GRS(GRS)/115SEM

LIBRARY OF CONGRESS CATALOGING-IN-PUBLICATION DATA
has been applied for.

ISBN 0-7534-5798-9

Printed in India

Contents

Chapter One

Captain Pepper wanted a pet—
but he didn't want a parrot.
"Every pirate I've ever
met has had a parrot,"
he said.
"Parrots talk too
much. No, I want
a pet that will
make me famous
all over the world."

"So let's go to the pet store," said Pirate Nong.

"Goldfish are best," said Pirate Noodle.

"Let's buy a hamster!" said Pirate Noddypoll.

"Silly fools!" roared Captain Pepper.
"A hamster or a goldfish won't make
me famous! What I want is something
different."

What Captain Pepper wanted
Captain Pepper got.

So off they sailed aboard the
Snooty Fox to search for a pet
that was different.

Chapter Two

The pirates sailed for many long

weeks.

At last they reached an island.

"Aha!" cried

Captain Pepper.

"I'll bet my

boots we'll find

my pet here. Full

speed ahead, you

horrible bunch!"

They sailed down a river and into
a jungle.

"Stop!" bellowed the Captain.

"Lower the gangplank and get ashore!
Find me a pet, or I'll feed you to the
sharks!"

Then Captain Pepper lay down
in his hammock for a nap.

"Come on," sighed
Pirate Nong.
"Let's find his pet, and
then we can go home."

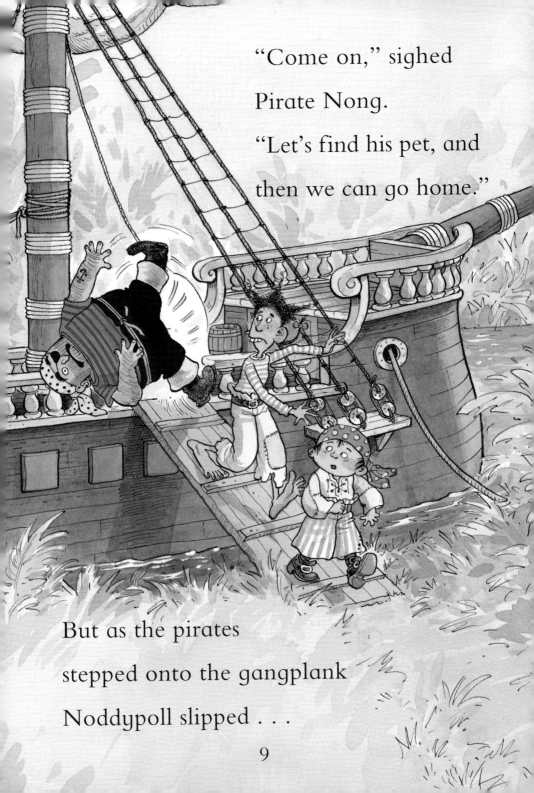

But as the pirates
stepped onto the gangplank
Noddypoll slipped . . .

9

and fell in the water.

"Help!" he screamed. "I can't swim!"

Suddenly a huge, toothy creature tossed
Noddypoll up in the air.

"Help!" he screamed. "I want my mom!"

Captain Pepper jumped
to his feet. "Bless my soul,
it's a hippopotamus!"
he shouted. "That
would make a good pet.
Bring it onboard!"

The hippo didn't want
to be brought onboard.
It snorted and stamped
and snapped at the
pirates.
But at last they
hauled it up
onto the deck.

"Welcome aboard, my hippo pet,"
said Captain Pepper.
"With you by my side, I'll soon be
famous all over the world."
He patted the hippo's head.

The hippo snorted . . .

and rushed across the ship.

CRUNCH!

It bit the mast in half.

CRASH!

The mast fell

onto the deck.

"Stop that now!" the Captain bellowed.

Captain Pepper glared at the hippo.

The hippo glared at Captain Pepper—

and charged!

Captain Pepper dived out of the way . . .

but the hippo kept going . . .

right over the side of the ship . . .

SPLASH!

"That hippo was trouble," said Pirate
Nong. "Can't we go home and buy
a parrot?"
Captain Pepper snorted and snarled.
"A parrot?" he roared. "Not on your
life! Find me something different,
or I'll feed you to the sharks!"

Chapter Three

The pirates set off into the jungle.

"The Captain should catch his own

pet," grumbled Noddypoll.

"Shhh!" said Nong.

"Look, by that tree! That's different."

A porcupine was scratching for grubs.

"It's black and white

like our pirate flag,"

said Nong.

"That would make a good pet for
Captain Pepper," said Noddypoll.
"Catch it, Noodle, before it runs off."
Noodle reached out his hand.

"Oww!" he squealed and leaped up
in the air. "Shiver me timbers!
It's covered in sharp things.
I'm not picking that up.
We'll find something else."
So on they went, tiptoeing slowly.

Suddenly something hit Noddypoll on the head.

"Ouch!" he howled. "Who's throwing things?"

The pirates looked up into the trees.

The monkey threw another
nut, and then it leaped to
the ground.

"That's different!" cried Nong.

"That would make a good
pet for Captain Pepper,"
said Noddypoll. "Catch it,
Noodle, before it runs off."

Noodle ran after the monkey, with
Noddypoll and Nong at his heels . . .

all the way back to the *Snooty Fox*.

"It's going onboard!" said Noddypoll.

The pirates chased the monkey up the gangplank and onto the ship.

The monkey jumped on the Captain's hammock and stole his hat.

Captain Pepper woke up from his nap.
"Stop!" he bellowed. "Give me back
my hat!"
The monkey climbed up the ropes
and swung on the sails.

"Get off my ship!" the Captain roared.

He waved his sword in the air.

SWISH! SWASH!

The monkey screeched and dropped the hat. Then it ran down the gangplank and disappeared back into the jungle.

"That monkey was trouble," said Pirate Nong. "Can't we go home and buy a parrot?"

Captain Pepper snorted and snarled. "A parrot?" he roared. "Not on your life! Find me something different, or I'll feed you to the sharks!"

Chapter Four

It was getting dark when the pirates set off into the jungle again.

Noddypoll clung to Noodle and whimpered.

"Shhh!" said Nong. "Look, over there."

"A kitty cat with spots! That's different," said Noddypoll.

"Catch it, Noodle, before it runs off."

"Here, kitty," called Noodle.

"Come to Noodle, good kitty."

The leopard crept
slowly toward him.

28

But the growl in its throat and the glint in its eye filled Noodle with fear.

"Shiver me timbers! He thinks I'm his dinner!" he cried.

Noodle turned and ran deeper into the jungle, with Noddypoll and Nong at his heels.

The jungle grew darker and even more scary.

On they went, tiptoeing slowly.

Then Noddypoll tripped over a fallen branch and landed on his bottom with a howl.

The branch began to wriggle.

"Aagh!" screamed Noddypoll.

"That branch is alive!"

"Well, shiver me timbers!" said Noodle.

"That's different!"

"Catch it, Noodle, before it runs off,"
said Noddypoll.

"It can't run," giggled Noodle.

"It's got no legs!"

He grabbed it by its middle and pulled.

"It's heavy," he cried. "You'll both
have to help."

Together the pirates carried the snake
through the jungle and back to
the *Snooty Fox*.

Captain Pepper couldn't believe his eyes.
"A python! You've brought me
a python!" he cried.
He hopped and skipped across the deck.
"I'm going to be famous!" he whooped.

Then Captain Pepper clapped his hands
and began to sing:
"Oh, a python is a wondrous thing,
No arms, no legs has he.
And yet he moves with lightning speed
To catch and eat with glee."

"We've found you a pet," said Nong.
"Can we go home now, please?"
Captain Pepper stopped singing.
"Go home?" he roared. "Not on
your life! We're going around the
world to show off my python.
I'm going to be famous!"
The pirates grumbled behind his back.
"We'll be off at daybreak," said the
Captain. "So you'd better be ready,
or I'll feed you to the sharks!"

Chapter Five

Daybreak came.

The pirates slept peacefully in their bunks.

At midday Nong woke up and stretched . . . "Something isn't right," he thought.

"Hey, wake up Noddypoll and Noodle," he called. "It's late. Why hasn't the Captain shouted at us?" The pirates crept up on deck and tiptoed toward Captain Pepper's hammock.

There were the Captain's boots . . .

There was the Captain's hat . . .

but there was no sign of Captain Pepper.

In his place, fast asleep, was

Captain Pepper's python pet—

with a large bulge in its middle.

"Where's the Captain?" cried

Noddypoll.

The pirates stared at the sleeping snake.

"I think *that's* the Captain," whispered

Nong, pointing to the bulge in the

python's middle.

"Well, shiver me timbers!" said Noodle.

Then suddenly Nong began to cheer.

"Now there's no one to shout at us!"

he cried.

"There's no one to feed us to the sharks!"

shouted Noddypoll.

"There's no one to stop us from going

home!" called Noodle.

The three pirates jumped for joy.

"First let's send Captain Pepper's pet back where it came from," said Nong. The pirates pulled back the hammock—HEAVE!

And let it go—
TWANNNNNG!

The python flew through the air—
WHEEE!—and back into the jungle.

"HOORAY!" shouted the pirates.
And they danced a merry dance all
around the deck.

Chapter Six

Noddypoll, Noodle, and Nong sailed back across the sparkling seas until at last they arrived home.

The three pirates sold the *Snooty Fox* for a fortune and bought a tea shop instead. On a perch in the tea shop window sat a parrot to welcome all the visitors.

As for Captain Pepper, his wish came true.

He soon became famous all over the world.

Captain Pepper was the only pirate in history to have been swallowed by his pet!

About the author and illustrator

Sally Grindley is an award-winning author,
and pirates are some of her favorite characters.
"I like writing about pirates because you can
make them as silly as you like," she says.
"And the crew in this story are definitely as silly
as any I have ever met!" Sally Grindley's other
books for Kingfisher include *What Are Friends For?*,
What Will I Do Without You?, and *Will You Forgive Me?*

David Parkins has illustrated many books for
children. "I love being an illustrator," he says, "but
running a tea shop sounds fun, too. I'd find it
difficult to resist all the cakes, though—especially
the treacle tarts!"

Strategies for Beginner Readers

Predict
Think about the cover, illustrations, and the title of the book. What do you think this book will be about? While you are reading think about what may happen next and why.

Monitor
As you read ask yourself if what you're reading makes sense. If it doesn't, reread, look at the illustrations, or read ahead.

Question
Ask yourself questions about important ideas in the story such as what the characters might do or what you might learn.

Phonics
If there is a word that you do not know, look carefully at the letters, sounds, and word parts that you do know. Blend the sounds to read the word. Ask yourself if this is a word you know. Does it make sense in the sentence?

Summarize
Think about the characters, the setting where the story takes place, and the problem the characters faced in the story. Tell the important ideas in the beginning, middle, and end of the story.

Evaluate
Ask yourself questions like: Did you like the story? Why or why not? How did the author make the story come alive? How did the author make the story fun to read? How well did you understand the story? Maybe you can understand it better if you read it again!